To Lorna and Gordon

Grandma
Copyright © 1992 by Alison Dexter
First published by ABC, All Books for Children,
a division of The All Children's Company Ltd., Great Britain.
Printed in Hong Kong. All rights reserved.
Typography by Francisca Galilea
1 2 3 4 5 6 7 8 9 10
First American Edition, 1993
The illustrations were created with
a combination of food coloring, pen and inks.
The text was set in 14/17 Kennerly Roman.

Library of Congress Cataloging–in–Publication Data
Dexter, Alison.
  Grandma / Alison Dexter.
    p. cm.
  "Willa Perlman books."
  Summary: Energetic Grandma romps at the beach with her
granddaughter and succeeds in wearing her out.
  ISBN 0-06-021143-1. — ISBN 0-06-021144-X (lib. bdg.)
  [1. Grandmothers—Fiction. 2. Beaches—Fiction.] I. Title.
PZ7.D5386Gr 1993   92–6473
[E]—dc20   CIP
                                                      AC

Alison Dexter
Grandma

 Willa Perlman Books

An Imprint of HarperCollinsPublishers

Every summer I go to stay
with Grandma.
   Grandma lives near the ocean.
   Mom and Dad give her strict
instructions to WEAR ME OUT!

At seven o'clock every morning
Grandma wakes me with classical
music and blackberry jam on toast.

By eight o'clock
she has cleaned
the whole
house . . .

. . . weeded
the vegetable
garden . . .

. . . done enough
baking for a
month . . .

. . . put on her best
dress and her pink
lipstick . . .

. . . and is
READY TO GO!

On our way to the beach we stop at the arcade. Grandma always gets "Highest Score—Play Again" on the high-speed driving games.

She says she had lots of practice when she and Grandpa used to go motorcycle racing.

At the beach we write our names in the sand, but Grandma makes one up. She doesn't like her real name (I don't blame her—it's Minnie).

I make a sand car, and we sit
in it until a huge wave comes in.

Grandma chases me with a crab,
but I get back at her with
some seaweed.

At the edge of the water,
Grandma holds up her skirt
so it won't get wet.

Then we rub the sand off
our feet, and I ask why one
of her little toes sticks out.
Grandma says that she was
barefoot once when she and
Grandpa were out dancing,
and her toe got caught in the
hem of his pants when they
spun in opposite directions.
It's never been the same since.

I am allowed to have ice cream, but
Grandma says definitely no bubble gum.

We go for a trip around the shore in an old fishing boat. It smells funny. Grandma wishes she'd brought her net so she could catch something for our dinner.

It's
a steep
walk home.

Grandma says it's easier if you go
sideways, like crabs on the beach.

When we get home,
I empty the sand out of
my socks and the shells
from my pockets.
    Then Grandma fills the tub
for my bath. I'm worn out!

The next morning, Grandma wakes me with classical music and blackberry jam on toast. Soon she will be ready to go—again!